Roland Wright
At the Joust

Don't miss these great books!

Roland Wright

#1 *Future Knight*

#2 *Brand-New Page*

Roland Wright
At the Joust

by Tony Davis

illustrated by Gregory Rogers

A Yearling Book

Text copyright © 2008 by Tony Davis
Cover art copyright © 2011 by James Madsen
Illustrations copyright © 2008 by Gregory Rogers

All rights reserved. Published in the United States by Yearling, an imprint of Random House Children's Books, a division of Random House, Inc., New York. Originally published in paperback in Australia by Random House Australia, Sydney, in 2008.

Yearling and the jumping horse design are registered trademarks of Random House, Inc.

Visit us on the Web! www.randomhouse.com/kids

Educators and librarians, for a variety of teaching tools, visit us at www.randomhouse.com/teachers

Library of Congress Cataloging-in-Publication Data
Davis, Tony.
At the joust / by Tony Davis ; illustrated by Gregory Rogers. — 1st Yearling ed.
p. cm. — (Roland Wright ; #3)
Summary: Roland, a scrawny, aspiring knight prone to hiccups, serving as a page in Twofold Castle, attends his first tournament, where knights from near and far take part in a full day of jousting.
ISBN 978-0-375-87328-7 (mass market original : alk. paper) —
ISBN 978-0-375-98925-4 (ebook)
[1. Knights and knighthood—Fiction. 2. Castles—Fiction. 3. Middle Ages—Fiction.]
I. Rogers, Gregory, ill. II. Title.
PZ7.D3194At 2011
[Fic]—dc22
2011007846

Printed in the United States of America

10 9 8 7 6 5 4 3 2 1

First Yearling Edition 2011

Contents

ONE. Sir Lucas   1

TWO. Morris Brings News   18

THREE. The Next King   35

FOUR. Hector's Surprise   46

FIVE. The First Joust   56

SIX. Expert Opinion   72

SEVEN. Little Douglas   81

EIGHT. Nudge's Decision   90

NINE. The Moment of Truth   102

TEN. An Heir Is Announced   116

One

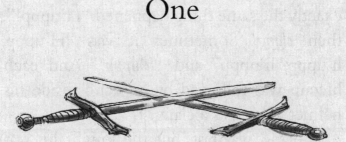

Sir Lucas

Roland Wright couldn't decide which was worse: the clanging great long-sword that kept crashing down on his helmet, rattling his teeth and threatening to cleave his head in two, or the hiccups.

Every time Roland lined up a good strike of his own, a bubble of air—or whatever it was—came flying up his windpipe and "H'uppp!", he missed.

Whenever he tried to defend himself, exactly the same thing happened. "H'uppp!", then *clang!* Sometimes it was "H'uppp, h'uppp, h'uppp" and *"h'uppp!"* And each hiccup was followed by an echo inside his helmet as well as a clang.

Roland was fast, but the knight he was facing was faster. Roland was strong for his size, but the other fighter was too—and he was a great deal bigger.

Roland's best defense was his ability to move his sword at lightning speed and block. However, that wasn't much good to him today. Even when he stopped the knight's sword, each blow was so mighty it just about knocked Roland out of his shoes.

Roland was ducking and weaving, slipping back and blocking. But he was still being hit hard and often.

"Ouch!" he would cry when his helmet clanged under the falling edge of a longsword.

Then "H'uppp!" Then "Arggh!" when his own attacking shot was blocked, then "H'uppp!" again as air rushed up his throat at the speed of a galloping horse.

Roland should never have eaten those grapes. And he should never have tried to fight this knight.

They were both using longswords, large, heavy weapons that were held with two

hands, meaning neither fighter had a shield.

Roland found it hard work even to lift his weapon, or to see out of his helmet. He was wearing bits and pieces of borrowed armor, some of it rusty, some of it very loose-fitting.

The knight swung his sword effortlessly and moved smoothly. He looked immaculate too, with a long white silk scarf around his neck and a helmet so shiny it sent sharp flashes of light through Roland's narrow eye slots.

So the newest page at Twofold Castle—the home of the noble King John—was squinting as well as hiccuping, as well as being hit in the helmet, as well as being struck on the body by an opponent who was older, larger and stronger.

He'd had better days. "Ouch! H'uppp! Arggh! H'uppp!"

Roland's pet white mouse, Nudge, was waiting nearby, in a cloth bag hooked over a tree branch. Nudge wasn't having much fun either, having been dropped on the ground earlier by a very nervous Roland. Nudge now had his paws pushed over his ears to block out the crashing, banging, smashing and walloping.

Roland slipped back again, out of range of the other longsword. He needed to remember what he'd been taught at the castle, to make sure he was fighting not just fiercely, but smartly.

Roland pointed his leading foot toward his target: the very top of the knight's helmet. He turned his back foot sideways for better balance. He kept his body straight and made sure his weight was on the balls of his feet. He changed his grip, holding his longsword tightly just behind the cross-guard with his stronger hand, his left hand. This meant he could swing more quickly. He also made sure his knuckles were perfectly lined up with the cutting edge, or the true edge, as the knights called it.

More importantly than any of that, Roland stuck out his bottom lip, as he always did when trying his very hardest. He moved in quickly, the longsword held high above his head. With the tip pointing at the sky, he thrust his arms as far forward as he could to create blade speed. At the last moment he cut down hard. For extra power, he stepped forward and shifted his weight to his front foot at exactly the same time.

As his blade swooped, Roland let forth a string of astonishing hiccups. "H'uppp, h'uppp, h'uppp, h'uppp . . . hhhh'uppp!" They echoed in his helmet—and probably in the surrounding hills too. But he didn't flinch, and his sword landed right in the middle of the knight's helmet, splitting in two the colorful plume on top.

It was a strike so hard that vibrations traveled right up Roland's arms. For the first time, he knew his opponent was in trouble.

The knight moved backward, a little unsteady on his feet. For a moment he looked to be falling. Then he straightened, marched back in, flicked his scarf away with his left hand and picked up the pace of his attack.

The knight swung his sword from above. He swung it from below, from the left side and the right. He twitched and twisted and turned it too, attacking not just with the true edge, but with the other side, known as the false edge.

At times the knight swung his blade behind him and struck with the pommel, the round weight at the end of the handle. *Doinggg!*

Roland realized the man in the dazzlingly

shiny armor and long white scarf had been taking it easy until now.

"Ouch! H'uppp! Arggh! H'uppp!" Roland blurted out. A *doinggg!* or two later, he was without his sword. It had been twisted from his hands by a winding movement so quick Roland had scarcely seen it. He could merely watch through the eye slots as his sword was flung into the distance.

Roland was hit yet again with the pommel—*doinggg!*—and found himself lying on the ground, looking up at a knight raising his longsword and preparing to bring it down like a spear.

For the first time, Roland was scared. Longswords could not easily pierce through steel in combat. But when a knight was on the ground and without any defense, a longsword could be thrust through a joint or any other weak part of the armor.

Roland looked up and saw the sword

flying down toward his visor. He closed his eyes, fearing that his last word on earth would be "H'uppp!"

Everything went black. The sword slid deeply and noisily into something. Roland hoped it wasn't him. After a moment he opened his eyes. He turned his head sideways and saw the sword sticking into the

grass. He then looked up to see the knight removing his helmet, pulling off the cloth arming cap he wore underneath and shaking his long brown hair.

"Hmmm, that's enough for today's lesson," the knight said, straightening his scarf. He had a thin mustache and eyes that were almost as green as the trees. "I only brought the sword down at the end to give you a scare—I thought it might cure your hiccups."

Roland slowly dragged himself to his feet, removed his own helmet and tried to shake the sweat off his face and out of his thick red hair. His ears were still ringing from all the blows to his helmet. He stood for a while, waiting for the next "H'uppp!", but it never arrived. "Thank you, Sir Lucas, I think I'm cured."

"That's good," said Sir Lucas after a pause. He always thought carefully before he said anything. "More grapes?"

"No thanks," said Roland, reaching instead for his leather water pouch.

Roland had been fighting Sir Lucas

on the meadow outside the north wall of Twofold Castle, with a dozen or so pages watching. One of the pages had long straw-colored hair and didn't seem able to stand still. He moved his weight from foot to foot as he watched the fight and spoke with the page next to him.

The page next to him was short and had straight black hair and a plump face. Two big dimples appeared whenever he smiled at what the first page was saying. That wasn't often, though, because the page with the black hair much preferred talking to listening.

The two boys were Humphrey and Morris, Roland's roommates. They had gasped when it looked as though Sir Lucas would stab Roland through the helmet, but now they were cheering.

"Bravo, Sir Lucas, bravo, Roland," yelled out Humphrey. "A terrifically good fight, a terrifically good fight." He tended to repeat his words when he was excited.

"Thanks, Sir Lucas, for curing the hiccups too," shouted Morris. "I wouldn't have slept tonight if Roland kept going 'h'uppp, h'uppp' and 'h'uppp!' It was even louder than Humphrey's snoring."

Sir Lucas used his arming cap to wipe sweat from his forehead, twirled one end of his thin mustache between thumb and first finger and then looked at Roland.

"Don't worry that you scored so few hits, Master Wright. I wanted you to learn where your weaknesses are so we can work on them. You did well, and next week we'll go back to theory and some simple exercises."

Sir Lucas then turned to the other page boys and adjusted his scarf. "The first time I saw this thin, freckly boy, he was fighting with a wooden sword. His speed and determination were remarkable. But the most impressive thing of all was his huge heart. There's no substitute for a huge heart. I thought: If a boy can fight so well without a lesson in his life, he'll be terrific with a bit of instruction. So I decided that whenever I had time, I would give him a lesson and see if there's anything I know that might help him. Because in this young boy, we have a champion of the future."

Sir Lucas's words raised a round of applause from all the boys on the meadow. Well, almost all. The one who didn't make a sound, other than a long hiss, was Hector. He was the oldest and tallest page—and the nastiest.

Hector shook his dark, bushy hair, ground his big teeth together and hissed a second time. Roland tried to ignore him. He took a couple more sips of water from his drinking pouch, walked to the nearby oak tree and opened his cloth bag.

"I did well," Roland said as Nudge ran up his arm and sat on his left shoulder. "Sir Lucas said so, and he's the most talented swordsman at the castle. I'm so lucky to be having lessons from him."

Roland peered at his shoulder and saw that Nudge wasn't as excited as he was. Nudge rubbed his black eyes, then gave one of his *I wish I could talk so I could tell you off* looks.

"Sorry about before," Roland said, stroking Nudge's back. "I didn't mean to drop you, and I didn't mean to tread on your tail when I was trying to pick you up."

"   ," Nudge replied grumpily.

As they walked back to the castle drawbridge, Roland realized with a start that it had been only a month since he left his small village to start a new life as a page. It felt like much longer.

Most things were going well. He had caught the attention of the King and the dashing young champion, Sir Lucas. But he had also caught the attention of Hector.

Roland had become comfortable in his page uniform, a tunic with large red and blue squares pulled tight by a thick black leather belt. And he had learned his tasks, such as serving at supper and helping the squires feed the dogs and horses.

Twofold Castle was an exciting place, and Roland's passion for all things knightly had grown stronger and stronger.

"Flaming catapults, Nudge," Roland said to his left shoulder. "I'm going to see a real battle or a siege soon, I can just feel it. Or maybe some jousting. Can you imagine anything half as exciting as jousting . . . except perhaps a full-scale war?"

Suddenly Roland's tone changed. "Oh dear, Nudge, here's Hector. He's been leaving us alone since he last got into trouble, but I think that's about to change."

Hector clomped up to Roland and Nudge and then waved his arm in a piece of mock chivalry. "After you, Roland *Wrong, s-s-s-s,* and your stinking rodent."

As he moved his hands back to his side, Hector "accidentally" clipped Roland's ear.

Roland quickly walked away and didn't look back. He didn't want to fight, and he didn't want Hector to think he'd upset him. But Hector had upset him.

Two

Morris Brings News

Ever since King John declared him "the official mouse of Twofold Castle," Nudge had been allowed to sleep in his elm-wood box at the end of Roland's bed.

He could even join Roland at the supper table. Nudge just had to be kept out of sight of Queen Margaret, who hated mice. Really hated them.

Humphrey and Morris now considered Nudge one of their roommates. They had found an old gauntlet, or steel glove, and bent it on a stone with a hammer to make it look a little—just a little—like a suit of mouse-sized armor.

"Nudge is here by royal appointment, royal appointment," said Humphrey, smiling as usual. "He needs his own battle dress in case he has to help defend Twofold Castle. Just in case, just in case."

Nudge's armor was very rough and weighed far more than Nudge did. But Roland proudly kept it next to the elmwood box. Just in case.

Roland had started his studies. His teacher, Chaplain Don, was very old and very strict, and there were far too many letters to learn.

The chaplain said schooling was absolutely necessary for anyone who wanted to be a knight. Roland wasn't sure why: you didn't have to be able to spell "slice" or "cut" or "stab" or "hack" to do it. And you didn't have to count up how many people you had slain on the battlefield, then add it to the number someone else had killed, then divide by some other silly amount. Even so, Roland was determined to try hard.

Because Humphrey was still struggling with his letters, the two boys agreed to help each other. They started work on a "page's alphabet" they could recite while fighting.

"A is for armor, shiny and *strong*," Roland said as he lifted his wooden sword high and brought it down hard.

"And B is for battle, bloody and *long*," Humphrey replied as he blocked and caught Roland's sword in a bind so that Roland couldn't strike.

"C stands for castle, high on the *hill*." Roland twitched his sword and struck it across Humphrey's shield.

"D for the dragons we one day shall *kill*," Humphrey replied. "And I've thought of another couplet on my own, another couplet. Listen:

"E is for effort, you must give your *all*, while F is for fighting, in melee or *brawl*."

"Bravo," said Roland. "If you stop hitting me for a moment, I'll try for the next one." Rhyming while fighting was hard to do at any time—and Roland was sore from the fight with Sir Lucas the day before.

"G stands for gauntlet, a steely great *glove*," Roland began, crunching up his forehead to think of a rhyme, ". . . and H for the hunting that all good knights *love*."

"You're becoming quite skillful at this, skillful at this," said Humphrey, pushing down Roland's sword and jabbing toward

his body. "Tomorrow we'll do I and J, and K and L, and maybe more. Maybe more."

Later that day, while Humphrey was busy with his chores, Roland walked across the bailey, the large open area inside the castle walls. He was daydreaming, as usual, and bumped into Morris.

"Ouch," said Roland, rubbing his nose and picking up Nudge, who had been dropped in the collision.

"I have the most amazing news,"

announced Morris, who didn't seem to notice that they had just banged heads. "There's a big tournament in a few days, and we're all going!"

"Flaming catapults, a real tourney!" Roland was suddenly hugely excited . . . until he stopped to think about it. Morris could sometimes overstate things just a bit.

"There will be jousting," gushed Morris, rubbing his mouth with the back of his hand. "And there'll be a dragon—a tame one that you can pat behind the ears, but that breathes real fire. And King Notjohn is sending across Sir Douglas, his tallest, strongest fighter, and he's going to take on one of us pages. He's so big they call him Little Douglas as a joke."

Nudge was too sore to share in the thrill of the news of the tournament. He quietly whimpered and gave Roland some very unpleasant looks.

"And," added Morris, "there will be thousands of knights who'll have a real battle and hundreds of them will be cut into tiny pieces."

Roland wasn't sure about any of it, yet there often seemed to be at least something true in Morris's stories. He had a way of finding things out.

"That's so exciting, Morris. The only tourney I've seen was a small practice one outside Sir Gallawood's castle. That was hand combat with just one joust at the end. And nobody had their head cut off or was run through with pikes."

"Well, you'll see all that here," Morris said as he ran his hand through his straight black hair. "This is the biggest tournament in the world."

The next day, Roland made his way toward the magnificent beast that lived in a wooden pen near the castle's western tower.

"How are you today, Mr. Elephant?" he said, looking over the top of the pen and into those big eyes. The elephant was a gift to the King from his brother, Notjohn—and had played a big part in Roland's short time at the castle. "Are you missing your family as much as I'm missing mine?"

While Nudge sniffed the air with his twitchy pink nose, Roland explained to the elephant—yet again—about his father, his older brother, Shelby, and his favorite oak tree back in the village. Roland didn't want to give up his new life. He just wished he could go home each night. Better still, he wished his father and brother could live at Twofold Castle and make the famous Wright Armor right here. And maybe bring the oak tree with them too.

"There's Sir Gallawood as well, Mr. Elephant. I miss his wise words, though I don't miss his punches in the shoulder. They're not nearly as funny as he thinks they are. I even miss Jenny Winterbottom a bit. She was the only person in the village the same age as me. I suppose I've already told you that."

Roland went quiet and thought about Jenny. She skipped a lot, and *tra-la-la*'d, and could be rather rude. And she thought she was *so* clever. But she was at least a little bit clever, and all right to play with when there were no boys around.

"Hmmm, Roland!" A nearby voice interrupted the daydream. It was Sir Lucas, who was talking to two other knights. They

were Sir Geoffrey and Sir Tobias, the long and the short of it, so to speak. The knights of Twofold Castle had returned with the

Queen from a distant tournament two weeks ago, and the jester had announced each of them in turn.

Roland remembered how the jester had called Sir Geoffrey a one-man army. He was by far the biggest knight in the castle. Even Sir Lucas came up only to his chin.

"Welcome home too, Sir Tobias," the jester had also said, shaking the bells on his shoes. "He's short, but a fine musician. Later he'll play you a Little Knight Music."

Sir Geoffrey had bright red hair, a big red mustache and a long scar down the side of his face. His shoulders were so wide that when Roland first saw him, he imagined his armor must have cost twice as much as anybody else's, since it had so much metal in it.

There would need to be lots of metal in his visor, too, because he had the longest, straightest nose Roland had ever seen.

Now Sir Lucas adjusted the crisp white scarf around his neck. "How are you, Nudge?"

"He's very well, thank you, sir," said Roland, while Nudge shook his head as if to say the complete opposite.

"I was just saying to these good men, Roland, that I've been looking at the King's Wright Armor—the very suit that saved his life. It's strong, and stylish, too. Perhaps I'll order some after the tourney."

"The tournament!" shrieked Roland. "It's true! Will there be jousting . . . real knights on real horses charging at each other with real lances? Will I be allowed to go?"

"There certainly will be jousting, and the horses and knights and lances will be real," said Sir Lucas. "But who goes is not a decision for me."

"I hear there's going to be a tame dragon," said Roland, "and a big knight named Little Douglas and a real battle in which hundreds of knights are going to have their gizzards sliced out."

Sir Lucas smiled. "I'm not sure about the dragon, or the exact size of Little Douglas. But I hope there aren't hundreds of knights left with their gizzards hanging out."

Sir Geoffrey nodded and pulled on the end of his long nose. Although a nod isn't a word, it was still as much as Roland had ever heard Sir Geoffrey say. The jester sometimes called him the Silent Knight.

"A tourney is about skill and bravery and horsemanship," Sir Lucas continued, twirling the end of his mustache. "And impressing the ladies, of course.

"It's more important to

be the best than to kill people. Even at the melee, the mock battle at the end, I hope nobody is seriously injured."

Roland wasn't sure whether to be happy or sad at this information. But he knew, as Nudge squeaked and chewed his collar, that he had more questions than he could ever ask. "Have you ever been unhorsed in a joust?" was the one that came straight out.

"Never," said Sir Lucas, with a rise of his shoulders. Sir Geoffrey merely shook his head and pulled on the end of his nose.

They both looked at Sir Tobias.

"Well, yes, *I've* been unhorsed." Sir Tobias's face was as scarred as Sir Geoffrey's. He had thick, curly white hair and wasn't a lot taller than Roland. But he was very wide and very strong. His shape reminded Roland of one of the sideboards in the Great Hall. Everyone seemed to like Sir Tobias. He moved slowly and gently but spoke more quickly than anyone Roland had ever heard. "It's happened three times, in fact. I'm not quite the champion that these men are. Nor as good-looking, for that matter."

"What's it like?" gulped Roland.

"Being unhorsed, or being ugly?" said the galloping voice of Sir Tobias. "Neither is very pleasant, but being unhorsed hurts more. The first thing you feel is an enormous thump, like you've been hit by a rock thrown from a catapult. You see nothing through your visor but blue sky.

"There's a second big thump when you hit the ground. Then all you see through your visor is grass. It takes quite a few moments before you know whether you've been badly hurt. Once a splinter from the other knight's broken lance went through my visor and stopped this far from my eye." Sir Tobias held up two short, thick fingers to show just how small the distance was. "I was very lucky.

"Though come to think of it," Sir Tobias added with a cheerful splutter, "it would have been luckier to have been born with talent, and to have won the joust in the first place."

Roland realized he should let the knights return to their knightly conversations. He excused himself and walked across the bailey with Nudge on his shoulder. "Imagine a splinter through the visor, Nudge! Imagine if I really did go to the tournament. Imagine if you came with me . . . and we met the dragon. Maybe *he'd* be scared of mice. The elephant certainly isn't."

Nudge was now a little happier. He stood high on his rear legs and his black eyes scanned the bailey.

"Imagine if we took part in the melee, Nudge, imagine if . . . Oh, look, they're reopening the drawbridge."

Roland often had hunches about things.

But he didn't suspect that what was going to happen next was going to happen next.

The noisy drawbridge slowly cranked down and reached the land on the other side of the green moat. Roland froze. He rubbed his eyes. Then he rubbed them again.

Nudge twitched his whiskers and rubbed his eyes too.

Three

The Next King

Roland and Nudge were staring straight at Sir Gallawood and Jenny Winterbottom.

Sir Gallawood was holding the reins of his horse in one hand and his helmet in the other. He saw Roland, but didn't smile. He looked hot and tired and very, very serious.

Jenny was thinner than Roland remembered, and paler. Her brown curls, which normally sprang out, hung limp. She walked with her shoulders slumped.

Roland pushed Nudge into his pocket and nervously ran up to meet them halfway along the drawbridge. "Hello, is everything all right?"

Sir Gallawood's voice was low and flat.

"Everything's fine with your family, Roland. Sadly, though, all's not so well elsewhere."

And with that, Jenny started sobbing. Sir Gallawood put his hand on her shoulder. "Jenny's mother choked on a fishbone. Everyone did what they could. I sent my own barber-surgeon, yet nothing could save her."

Sir Gallawood was dressed in his long green tunic with a coat of mail underneath. He had a sword in his belt and an arming cap on his head. His pointy black beard was filled with dust and dirt from the long trip.

"I feel a responsibility toward the people in the village below my residence," Sir Gallawood said. "I have no lady of my castle, so I have come to ask the King to take Jenny to be trained as a maid with one of the ladies here. I feel Jenny would be better off where she knows at least one person—a good person like you, Roland. We shall wait and see what His Majesty says."

Roland was still in shock that afternoon when he had his first music lesson. He thought he would be taught the lute, but instead he was handed a long stick and a stringed instrument with a straight neck and a polished wooden body the shape of half a pear.

"What is this, Lady Mary?"

"It's a rebec, Roland," she said, smiling from beneath the pointed wimple that sat on her head. Roland was her "special page," and it was her job to teach him culture and manners and music. "You play it with the long wand, the bow. I chose it for you because I think it sounds beautiful."

The rebec's neck felt slippery in Roland's hand. It had three thick strings made from the gut of an animal, and they hurt Roland's fingers when he pressed them against the fingerboard.

The bow was strung with horsehair and sometimes it hissed on the strings. *S-s-s-s!* It reminded Roland of a certain page with a big mouth and a sharply sloping forehead. *S-s-s-s.* Roland couldn't help but pull an ugly face whenever he heard the noise.

Lady Mary had a beautiful speaking voice, and bone-colored skin. She was a real lady, and Roland knew she deserved better than to see him pull ugly faces, or to hear him make an unholy racket.

"Playing an instrument well takes a great deal of practice," said Lady Mary softly as Roland squeaked and hissed and clunked and Nudge put his paws over his ears. "In that sense, it's just like swordsmanship."

"But swordsmanship is fun."

"Playing the rebec will also be fun in time. Already you are improving a little."

Roland was reminded how kind Lady Mary was. He knew if he had improved at all during his first lesson, he had merely gone from making the rebec sound like an animal in pain to making it sound like an animal in slightly less pain.

Still, a short time later, with Lady Mary urging him on, Roland managed to produce one perfect note. It was clean and sweet and seemed to hang in the air and make Roland think, all at once, of his family and friends, his sadness and good fortune, and of Jenny, now all alone in the world.

With that one long, beautiful note amid all the noise, Roland decided that maybe, just maybe, music could be worth learning.

Though, of course, it could never be as much fun as fighting.

After the lesson, Roland sprinted to the meadow. He had agreed to practice swords with Humphrey and Morris. When Roland arrived, Morris was facing a page with brown hair that curved up at the bottom like a helmet. Every time they looked ready to start fighting, Morris had one more thing to say.

Roland wasn't going to stand around. He ran straight toward Humphrey, wooden sword on high. "You will die, Sir Humphrey. You're no match for Sir Roland."

Humphrey cleverly blocked the downward thrust. "Maybe so, but you can't kill me until we make it to the end of our alphabet, to the end of our alphabet."

Roland wound his sword free, then held up his hand to stop the fight. Roland, after all, wasn't as good as Humphrey at fighting

and rhyming at the same time, and he had a lot else on his mind.

"I is for iron, the stuff of chain *mail*," he said, "and J is for . . . J is for . . . Jenny . . . Jenny Winterbottom, who arrived at the draw-bridge earlier today."

"That doesn't rhyme," said Humphrey. "And the J should be about jousting or something exciting, something exciting. Not about some person named Jenny."

"I know, Humphrey, but this is such a big surprise. My old neighbor just arrived at the drawbridge, along with the knight who lived closest to my village."

"Oh," said Humphrey, looking far more interested in a witty couplet than in Roland's old neighbor or closest knight. "I'll try it myself, try it myself:

"I is for iron—to make a mail *vest,* and J is for jousting, the ultimate *test.*"

Roland stuck out his bottom lip and tried to come up with something to follow. But his mind was as tangled as a bucket of worms. Would Jenny be able to stay? Would that be a good thing? If she stayed, could others from his village come too? Would Roland see more of Sir Gallawood before he left for Gallawood Castle? And why did he keep asking himself questions?

Suddenly a rhyme just tumbled out of Roland's mouth. "K is for knight, though it should start with N, L's for Sir Lucas, who'll outfight ten *men*."

"That's a cheat!" Humphrey said with a smile—and a wild swipe of his sword that Roland only just managed to duck under. "The L should be something like lance, something like lance. Anyway, Sir Lucas starts with an S. . . ."

"I meant the Lucas, not the Sir," said Roland as he advanced, then stabbed his opponent's shield, "and I really admire him."

The two roommates continued to chase each other up and down the meadow. Humphrey tried everything to get past Roland's speedy sword but without success. After a while Roland yelled out. "How about this one instead:

"K is for king: a man strong, brave and *wise* . . ."

Roland paused for a moment or two, trying to think of the follow-up. Suddenly he felt a long stick jabbing him right between the ribs. It was Hector, who had appeared out of nowhere.

"And L's for a longsword, *s-s-s-s*, to poke through your *eyes*!"

Four

Hector's Surprise

"**Y**our lesson today will have no letters or numbers," croaked the impossibly old gray-haired chaplain. "Instead we have a special guest who has something important to tell you."

With that, the door burst open and a short man with a huge stomach strutted in. He was dressed in a bright blue coat with gold braiding and wore brown shoes with buckles so shiny the reflections made patterns on the ceiling. The sword in his belt rubbed on the ground as he walked. The pages might have laughed if he didn't look so serious.

"My name is Urbunkum, Lord Urbunkum," the man said in a high-pitched, echoing voice. "But, boys, please feel free to call me Your Most Gracious and Worthy Honor.

"As you might know—as you *should* know—I'm the King's expert."

Lord Urbunkum seemed to puff up to twice his normal size when talking about himself. "I train the knights in warcraft, jousting, chivalry, sword fighting and, above all, in achieving excellence. Which is to say, I help them be better in every part of their lives."

With those words, his blotchy red face glowed and the small clumps of hair on his forehead and above each ear stood at attention. "I'm a Very Important Person at

Twofold Castle, and very busy. But if you ever need advice on anything at all, you'd be best to ask me."

When he wasn't talking, the Very Important Person coughed every few seconds, as if to draw notice to himself. "Today I'm not here to tell you how to make your own small lives better, but to talk about a tournament the pages will attend."

"Yes!" shrieked Roland above the cheers of Morris, Humphrey and the other boys in the class. "It's true, we're going to a tourney!"

The chaplain looked at Roland sternly. Lord Urbunkum produced a few more small coughs before saying, "And, boys, this will be history in the making. For the first time ever, a tournament will be used to choose the next King."

The room went silent while the boys tried to work out what this meant. Again, it was Roland who spoke first.

"But when the King dies, doesn't the throne just go to his oldest son, Prince Daniel?"

The chaplain looked at Roland even more sternly, but the King's expert smiled.

"That certainly was the case," Urbunkum said, placing his hands on his massive stomach and looking terribly proud of himself. "However, a short while ago I humbly suggested to His Majesty that the position of heir should go to whoever is best for the job.

"His Majesty agreed. Therefore, the King's twenty-four senior knights will compete in a series of jousts. Only when all the combat is complete and everyone's performance has been carefully measured, *only then* will we select the King's oldest son, Prince Daniel."

"Oh," said Roland, scratching his head. "That doesn't seem right."

The chaplain gave Roland yet another severe glance. Lord Urbunkum looked at

Roland as if he was the stupidest person in the world.

"Do you think, young man, that we should just appoint the King's firstborn son without at least making it look fair? It's *that* that wouldn't seem right."

The Very Important Person explained that the pages would attend the tournament at his suggestion. They would help the squires, watch, learn—and listen to Lord Urbunkum address the knights.

"I will be an inspiration to you all," he said.

As they walked from the classroom, Morris smiled his big dimply smile. "I told you we were going. What I didn't tell you is that the tame dragon will fight the elephant, and the loser will be served up as part of the feast they have at the end of every tournament."

Roland was shocked and hoped it wasn't true. But he didn't have long to think about it. As soon as they reached a grassy part of the bailey, Humphrey ran up to Roland with his wooden sword on high. Roland was ready not just with a blocking move, but with a couplet he had already worked out:

"M is for mace, to be swung with great *might,* and N is for Nudge, the smallest white *knight.*"

"Not bad," said Humphrey. "But I have a better one than that, better one than that.

"M is for mace, to be swung till they *flee,*"

he yelled, rushing in again with his sword. "And N is for no one, 'cause that's who'll beat *me*."

Roland slipped back, not to defend himself from the blow, but to think of the next letters—and a good rhyme.

At that moment Jenny appeared. There were tears in her eyes. She ran up to Roland and threw her arms around him, squashing Nudge, who was lying in his top pocket.

"They said *yes*! I'm to be trained as a maid, to help Lady Mary."

Nudge whimpered and, when scooped out, gave Roland—and Jenny—the foulest glare.

"I just wish my mother could see me now," added Jenny, wiping her eyes. "Lady Mary said I could perhaps one day become a lady-in-waiting."

"Does that mean," Morris interrupted,

"that you're a lady-in-waiting to be a lady-in-waiting?"

Jenny turned to Morris, glared at him and breathed out in disgust. "I won't be waiting on you, no matter what happens."

For one of the few times in his life, Morris found himself with nothing else to say. He slinked away.

"Who's this?" Humphrey asked Roland.

"A little lady friend of yours, a little lady friend?"

"She's not a friend," Roland said a bit too forcefully. "She's a neighbor. Well, she was a neighbor."

Roland was embarrassed. He felt sorry for Jenny, now she was an orphan. But he wasn't sure he wanted her at Twofold Castle all the time. And he certainly didn't want anyone calling her his lady friend.

How unlikely it all was: two of them from the same little village living in the King's castle, and both linked to Lady Mary.

"I have to go," Roland mumbled. He walked back across the bailey, lost in his thoughts. Jenny, the tourney and the elephant were all passing through Roland's mind when Humphrey ran up, swinging his sword.

"Not so fast! You still owe me two more letters, two more letters."

Roland clenched his fists, stuck out his bottom lip and yelled triumphantly, "O is for outlaws, to chase and to *strike,* P's for a pole-axe, a page and a *pike.*"

That left Humphrey with Q and R. He shook his long blond hair, scratched his head, then smiled broadly and began to speak. Roland never heard Humphrey's couplet, however, because Hector again barged in and talked over the top of it.

"This tournament is going to be exciting, *s-s-s-s.* Do you know why, you little red-headed squirt? Because I've organized a surprise for you. Ha, ha, ha."

Five

The First Joust

"Flaming catapults, Nudge!" Roland knew no other expression that summed up what he could see. Except perhaps "Fry my gizzards."

There were more suits of armor and more weapons than he had seen in his whole life. They gleamed in the sun so brightly that at times Roland had to cover his eyes.

There were more horses than Roland

had seen in one place too. Some were being watered or fed; others were being led around the tournament field, clopping along proudly like royalty. Almost all the horses were wearing brightly colored cloth trappers splashed with the colors of their knights.

There were pennants tied to lances that had been thrust into the ground. They flapped in the breeze outside the arming tents, where the knights would don their armor and prepare their weapons. These tents were also decorated with colors and emblems. The whole field was awash with reds, blues, golds and purples, and dragons, eagles, griffins, suns and crosses.

Roland's nostrils were filled with the scent of freshly ripped-up grass, earth and the newly sawn wood used to build a long barrier down the middle of the lists—the field where the jousting would soon take place.

There was the aroma of cooked meat too,

with large plates of it being carried toward the royal tents along with enormous jugs of ale.

Sir Geoffrey was practicing on a nearby hill. Twofold Castle's biggest knight wore a fancy helmet with a huge red plume on top. He rode a fine white horse and dropped the tip of his lance with each burst of speed. The noise of his charging carried across the fields.

Roland walked up to an arming tent. He knew the coat of arms—a leaping white unicorn against a gold background—and recognized the squire who was polishing the armor and arranging a selection of new white silk scarves. It was Sir Lucas's tent, though there was no sign of the man himself.

Despite his excitement, Roland sensed that something was not quite right. It was nothing to do with Hector's surprise, though that was a worry. It was to do with Sir Lucas.

Alongside the tent was a rack with a

dozen spare lances, each painted gold and with a little unicorn on the handle. Sir Lucas must have been confident he would break

many lances against the armor of his opponents. Yet Roland's stomach produced an uneasy stirring.

His stomach kept twisting and turning as he walked onto the lists. It felt no better when he looked up at the row of raised seats where the King, Queen and other important people would sit and watch the competition.

"Roland!" It was Sir Gallawood. "Exciting stuff, isn't it?"

"My first proper tourney," Roland said with an uncertain smile.

"I thought I'd stay on after delivering young Jenny Winterbottom, so I could see the King's best knights in combat. I think it will be terrific."

"I think so too, Sir Gallawood, but you'll need to tell me how it all works."

"Of course, Roland. Ah, look—here comes the Queen."

Roland stood to attention as Sir Galla-wood added under his breath, "She always insists on handling her own horse."

Queen Margaret swept into the grounds, and Roland immediately pushed Nudge into his top pocket. The Queen's long dark hair trailed behind her as she raced along side-saddle on a magnificent brown and white stallion—which she rode straight into the side of an arming tent.

"Arrrrhh!" the Queen growled in a most unqueenly way as she slid off the horse and bounced across the low roof of the tent.

A loud "Ouch!" came from inside the canvas walls, and a knight in his under-garments ran out. He began to shout at who-ever had stupidly barreled into the side of his pavilion, but then he realized who it was.

"Your Majesty," he said, changing his tone. "My most gracious Queen Margaret ..."

The knight began bowing, while trying

to cover himself up. "I can but most humbly apologize, Your Majesty, for so carelessly putting my inconsequential structure in your path."

Sir Gallawood rolled his eyes and gave Roland a friendly punch to the shoulder that almost knocked him into the nearby barrier.

"The knights have been split into two

teams, Roland, just like in a battle. Sir Lucas, Sir Geoffrey, Sir Tobias and nine others are in the Tenans, and the other side is known as the Venans.

"The knights will joust for their teams, and their points—or number of broken lances—will be added together at the end. A winning side will be announced. More importantly, an individual champion will be declared—a new heir to the throne."

Roland looked across to see foot servants, who had been breathlessly running behind the Queen, help her climb down from the roof of the tent and remount. Her Majesty then turned her horse around and knocked over a herald who was unrolling his scroll to announce her arrival.

As always, Roland had a million questions. "What is the long barrier in the middle of the lists, Sir Gallawood?"

"A good question, Roland. It is a very

new idea. It's called a tiltline and keeps the jousting knights apart as they run toward each other.

"At my last tournament there was no such barrier. Two jousters ran straight into each other, killing their horses and badly injuring themselves."

"What about the dragon?" gushed Roland. "The tame one that breathes real fire?"

"I haven't seen him," replied Sir Galla-wood, looking befuddled. "Maybe he had somewhere more exciting to go."

A short while later Roland saw Sir Lucas, and that queasy feeling returned. Sir Lucas had a longsword in hand and a fresh white scarf wrapped around his neck. He was step-ping and passing and stepping and passing, as if taking part in a dance.

"Do you still need to practice your foot-work, Sir Lucas?"

The knight took his time to answer, as

usual. "Hmmm. Of course, Master Roland, I perform exercises every day to make sure I'm in top form for longswords, rapiers, lances, the melee, jousting or any other form of combat.

"The best-prepared man has a big advantage, Roland, and ladies appreciate it too."

"Sir Lucas, you will be safe, won't you?" Roland had never before worried about such things. But then, he'd never seen someone he knew well fight in a dangerous competition.

Sir Lucas smiled and flashed his green eyes as he stepped and passed and stepped and passed. "I was chatting to Sir Gallawood on that subject. He says he has ordered a suit of Wright Armor and will receive it in a few months. I told him that I too shall order some."

"Fry my gizzards!" said Roland. "I could go to the village with you, sir, and help you, and see my father and Shelby."

"Hmmm, that would be good." Step, pass, step, pass.

Thoughts of the village set Roland off on another daydream. He imagined himself sitting down to a meal with his father and brother. He was telling them of his adventures, but also listening to his father explain what had been happening in the village, and hearing Shelby say how much he enjoyed training as an armorer.

With Nudge on his shoulder, and still lost in his thoughts, Roland wandered through the rows of tents and past a line of trumpeters readying to announce the first contest. He wished he could be taking this walk with his father and brother. He imagined too that he was a jouster, and that his father and brother were here to see Roland Wright declared champion . . . maybe even the heir to the throne.

"Oops . . . sorry!" Roland had walked

straight into the legs of Sir Tobias, who was sitting on a very wide chair outside his arming tent. Roland fell flat on his face, but for once his pet mouse didn't share his pain. Nudge managed to jump off just before Roland hit the ground.

"Hello, Roland; hello, Nudge," said Sir Tobias, rubbing his right knee and talking at the speed of a flying arrow. "You're probably wondering why I'm not practicing my footwork, sword swings or lance grips."

"In truth," said Roland, spitting out blades

of grass, "I was daydreaming about my family."

Nudge watched Roland pull yet more grass off his tongue, and let out what sounded like a mouse-sized giggle.

"As it turns out, I'm just catching up on my reading," Sir Tobias said, holding up a large and weighty book and gently shaking his curly white hair. "Knights need to be studious and clever, as well as brave and strong. Although maybe, of course, I'm none of them. This is called *Slay a Dragon a Day*, but there's quite a lot about lance work in here.

"Lance work is what we'll be doing first up. So if I read this properly, when I get beaten I'll know what I did wrong."

Roland spat out what he hoped was the last of the greenery. "*Slay a Dragon a Day*? Isn't that by Lord Urbunkum?"

"That's right," said Sir Tobias. "Once we

thought we could get by without an expert. But as the King says—or is it the expert himself?—the time that people like us waste doing things is the time Lord Urbunkum spends studying how those things can be done better."

Sir Tobias picked up a flute and turned his eyes back to the book. He played just a few slow notes as he read, but the melody was so pure and charming that people all around stopped what they were doing to listen.

Among those drawn to the music were Lady Mary and Jenny. "A good day to you, sir, and best of luck in the jousts," Lady Mary said when Tobias had finished playing his little air. "I should introduce Jenny Winterbottom, newly arrived at the castle and soon to be trained as a maid. Roland is a friend of hers."

Jenny looked at Sir Tobias. "He's not a friend," she said as the sound of two horses running at each other filled the air. "He's a neighbor.

"Well, he was a neighbor," she added above the almighty *thwack!* of a lance breaking against armor.

"We're missing the first joust," screeched Roland. "Nudge—let's go!"

Roland ran to the lists in time to see Sir Geoffrey jumping off his horse with a broken lance still in his hand. Halfway along the tiltline another knight lay on the ground, squirming with pain. Sir Geoffrey threw down the lance and ran toward him.

"A victory to the Silent Knight," bellowed the King's constable, who seemed to be in charge of the tournament as well as the castle. "He has unhorsed his opponent on the first pass," the constable added with his huge rusty-hinge voice.

Roland sighed. "Nudge, how silly to be talking when we could have been watching Sir Geoffrey joust so brilliantly for the Tenans."

As Roland and Nudge watched the knight from the Venans carried from the lists, a voice sounded from very close behind.

"That man's in better shape, *s-s-s-s,* than you'll be in by the end of the day, *peasant boy.*"

Six

Expert Opinion

Roland watched spellbound as one knight after another galloped down the tiltline, smashing his lance into splinters against his opponent's armor.

He saw the Tenans gain the upper hand. He saw the Venans fight back. He even saw two knights drop their lance tips in perfect unison and knock each other off their horses at exactly the same time. They ended up sitting on the grass a few yards from each other, dizzily trying to work out what had happened.

Roland loved the pounding on the grass as the knights charged, the sun bouncing off the helmets and the shouting of the crowd when lance hit shield or armor.

Between the jousts, though, were long speeches that Roland could have done without. And just when Sir Lucas was about to fight for the first time, Roland was called away to help a squire move an arming tent from the route the Queen was expected to follow home. He ran back to hear that Sir Lucas had won, though only just.

"Maybe my hunch was wrong, Nudge," he whispered to his pocket as Sir Geoffrey prepared to joust again.

Roland watched the charge, the crash and the people in the raised seats clapping and shouting as the knight from the Venans twisted in his saddle and somehow managed to stay on his horse.

"Flaming catapults, Nudge!" Roland said as Sir Geoffrey threw away his broken lance and called for a new one. "Did you see how hard he hit him? What skill! What power! Go, Tenans!"

Sir Geoffrey broke his lance twice more. But in the third and final pass the other knight broke his, too, so the final score was three lances to one. It was good to see Sir Geoffrey win again, but Roland was really waiting for just one thing: Sir Lucas's next joust.

It was against Sir Sterling, a knight Roland didn't really know. Fortunately, if points were given for looking good, Sir Lucas had the upper hand. The corner of his white scarf stuck out from the bottom of his helmet, and the sight of the unicorn and gold on his shield, surcoat and horse's

trapper made Roland feel much more confident.

Mind you, Sir Sterling wore the whitest armor Roland had ever seen, and the front of his helmet was completely smooth except for the tiniest slit for his eyes. A tall green feather was mounted on top to match the green background on Sir Sterling's crest of arms.

"I'm nervouser than ever before, Nudge,"

Roland said, and then sighed when he realized there'd be a further delay. Yes, it was another speech, this time by Lord Urbunkum.

"Your Majesty King John, Your Majesty Queen Margaret, honored knights, ladies and gentlemen." Lord Urbunkum stood at the side of the lists and puffed out his chest. "As the King's personal expert, I've been developing improved techniques for all situations, including jousting.

"In earlier bouts I examined Sir Lucas's brave but unscientific style. I have now explained to him that he needs to fight differently—and hold the lance differently— if he's to achieve true excellence."

Lord Urbunkum coughed a few times, then added, "Those of you who admired Sir Lucas's narrow victory earlier today are now going to see something truly special."

Sir Lucas adjusted his scarf with his

gauntlet, then winked at Roland and dropped his visor. But even to someone who knew as little about jousting as Roland, Sir Lucas looked uncomfortable. He was holding his lance out farther from his body than normal.

"Come on, Sir Lucas. Go, Tenans!" chanted Roland nonetheless. "Knock Sir Sterling off his horse, knock him to kingdom come!"

The crowd went silent. All that could be heard was the snorting of horses, the flapping of flags, banners and pennants, and some hammering from an arming tent where a helmet was being repaired.

"This is the bout many of us have been waiting for," the constable yelled, with his big black eyebrows and mustache bouncing up and down in time with the words.

"Between two knights with the best statistics in the sport. A matching of power and accuracy . . . a contest that will surely bring us closer to finding our champion."

Sir Lucas's nervous horse moved away from the end of the tiltline. It wouldn't line back up, and Sir Lucas had to complete several turns to calm it down.

While Nudge chewed a small piece of splintered lance, Roland smiled toward Lady Mary, who was sitting in the stands, and Jenny, who was leaning against them. It was to say, "This is my special knight and he's going to win in fine style."

Roland just hoped he was right.

At last Sir Lucas lifted his lance to signal he was ready. The horses charged noisily. Both men dropped their lance tips from on high at the last moment to create extra thrust, and they hit each other's shields right in the middle. *Thumpppp!*

Both their lances broke, to the huge cheer of the crowd. On the second pass it happened again, but Sir Lucas was almost pushed off

the back of his saddle. He writhed with pain as he made his way to the end of the tiltline to turn for his third and final pass.

Sir Lucas looked very unsettled, and Roland still didn't like the way Urbunkum had made him hold his lance. Nudge paced up and down nervously, while Roland's stomach churned. It wasn't meant to be like this.

The third pass created the biggest impact of the day. Roland watched Sir Sterling's lance hit just above Sir Lucas's shield and slide toward his helmet. From then, it all seemed to slow down.

Sir Lucas was thrown up and backward. Roland and Nudge watched openmouthed as he slowly rolled and twisted a full three yards above the grass. He began to fall, head-first, crashing his helmet against the tiltline.

Twofold Castle's newest page shrieked at the sound of Sir Lucas's armor rattling to the ground. Roland ran out onto the lists to help, but was pulled away by one of the tournament guards. He saw Lady Mary lift her silk handkerchief to her face in horror. He heard Jenny scream. And he noticed Lord Urbunkum leaving so quickly he scarcely had time to cough.

Seven

Little Douglas

The spectators boldly cheered Sir Sterling's fine hit. But after a while they became quiet when they realized that a brave and popular knight had been badly injured.

Sir Sterling leapt off his horse and ran to the spot where Sir Lucas lay broken. He was following the code of chivalry: one knight must never leave another to die of his injuries.

Sir Lucas's squire and others also arrived. Together they carried away the motionless knight. Even the constable looked upset as he walked out to speak.

"A victory to Sir Sterling," he said in a slightly quavering voice as the sun glinted off his bald head. "He has unhorsed his opponent on the third pass."

Roland ran to Sir Lucas's arming tent, but a big hand grabbed his page's tunic and stopped him from going in.

"Calm down, young man," said Sir Gallawood, who was now holding Roland's shoulders tightly. "No one else is allowed in. But they have the best people working on him." Roland slumped to his knees as Sir Gallawood added, "With a bit of luck, he'll be fighting fit and back on his horse later in the day."

After what he'd seen, Roland didn't think Sir Lucas would be fit for fighting, or for any other thing, any time soon.

Roland wandered away with everything blurred by tears. He rubbed Nudge's back and walked nowhere in particular. When people talked, he didn't really try to hear what they were saying. A couple of times he banged into a fence or tripped over a tent rope.

After a while Roland felt an arm around his shoulder. He kept walking but eventually looked across to see the hazy outline of a face. It was Jenny Winterbottom. He waited for her to say something, but as his view improved, he realized she too was crying.

Roland knew that she felt exactly as he did: a long, long way from home, in a very strange world where nothing happened quite the way you expected. She had lost her mother, and now Roland might have lost the knight who had shown so much faith in him. He couldn't believe that any of it was happening.

After a while they sat on the grass together, Jenny's arm still around Roland's shoulder. The tournament continued noisily in the background, but neither of them was the slightest bit interested.

With Nudge nuzzling against his neck, Roland reflected that Sir Lucas hadn't been wearing Wright Armor. Maybe his father's armor could have made the difference. He feared he'd never go back to his village with

Sir Lucas, and never have another lesson from the most skillful swordsman he had ever known.

Roland noticed a shadow move across his face and felt a kick in the ankle. "The little *peasant boy, s-s-s-s,* has found a little *peasant girl,* I see. And she's just as big a crybaby as he is."

Roland looked up to see Hector smiling broadly. "Don't forget, *s-s-s-s,* my surprise. . . . Ever heard the name Little Douglas? Ha, ha, ha."

Tournaments didn't seem like nearly so much fun after all.

The jousts went on, but Roland didn't watch. He heard the noise of the melee, but he stayed sitting with Jenny and Nudge. Roland scarcely felt anything at all when the team he had cheered for—the Tenans—was declared the victor.

Soon afterward, there was a short blast of trumpets and the constable shouted, "All pages present themselves now!"

Humphrey, Morris and the others walked toward the lists, and eventually Jenny gave Roland a gentle push and he dragged his heels behind them.

Standing beside the constable was

a knight who looked even thinner than Roland and not much taller. He was wearing a breastplate, a shirt of mail and a helmet with a full visor. No one could see his face.

His sword was almost as tall as he was, but he swung it with great speed and skill. There were gasps all around; none of the pages had ever seen such a small person display such fancy moves.

"Is it a man or a boy, a man or a boy?" asked Humphrey.

"Has to be a man," said Morris. "He's far too quick and strong."

The constable shouted again over the muttering of the pages. From this close, his voice was so loud and raspy some of the pages jumped backward in fright, and Nudge curled into a little ball.

"It's my pleasure to announce that His Majesty King Notjohn—ruler of all the conquered lands—has sent Little Douglas to this tournament."

Roland and Humphrey looked at Morris. Could this be Little Douglas? Had he been given his name not because he was big, but because he was, well, *little*?

"King Notjohn says Little Douglas is the best fighter of his height in the known world," said the constable. "He is very slight and, at eleven and a half, still a page. However, Little Douglas has never been beaten, even by King Notjohn's best squires.

"By agreement between the two Kings, he is to be matched against the best page from Twofold Castle as a special entertainment for the ladies."

There were more mutterings from the gathered pages. They looked at each other, wondering who Twofold Castle's "best page" was.

"Choosing the challenger," rasped the

constable, causing more pages to jump backward, "is the responsibility of King John's
oldest page."

Roland turned around and looked at
Hector, who was now dressed more like a
squire than a page. Hector hissed, then smiled
at Roland.

At another time Roland might have
been worried, or excited, or confused. Right
now, he felt nothing. He didn't care what
happened to him, as long as Sir Lucas was
all right.

Eight

Nudge's Decision

"**G**ood afternoon, page boys," Hector said, spitting out the words "page boys" like an insult.

"When I was preparing to speak today, I thought it was best to change from my page uniform, *s-s-s-s,* and to put on a new white shirt.

"It's to remind you that I'm different from the rest of you. I'm older and more experienced. I'm also more important, *s-s-s-s,* because my father owns thousands of acres and has his own army."

Hector stood up straight and proud. "As for Little Douglas, obviously *I'm* the best page from Twofold Castle. I could beat him myself in an instant, *s-s-s-s,* and I'd scarcely raise a sweat. On this occasion, though, I'd rather see our newest page boy fight.

"Roland Wright is a reasonable swordsman. Pity then, *s-s-s-s,* there'll be no swords in the fight." Hector laughed and hissed and laughed and hissed. "Pity too that he's left-handed."

The constable sent Roland to a nearby tent to dress, telling him to hurry. But Roland walked slowly, lost in a daze.

"I can't fight," he whispered to the mouse cradled in his arm. "I'm too upset, and I don't even know what we're supposed to be fighting with."

"   ," said Nudge, turning his head to one side and rubbing his paw gently against the inside of Roland's wrist.

"And what, Nudge, has being left-handed got to do with anything?"

Roland and Nudge made their way to the tent. Inside was a large wooden box overflowing with mail and breastplates and shields and helmets and visors. Roland slumped to the floor and held Nudge.

After a while Humphrey burst in. "Off the floor. We've come to help you, come to help you."

"Yes," added Morris, following closely behind and rubbing his hand over his mouth.

"We know you're upset, but I heard Little Douglas say how scared he was of you . . . and I wanted you to know that."

"He did not," snapped Roland. "He doesn't even know who I am. Go away, both of you."

"We're not leaving," said Morris. "You're our friend."

"Quite right," said Humphrey, dancing around with his hair swinging from side to side. "We would have been here earlier, would have been here earlier, but we went

to find out what you'll be fighting with. They said lances. Lances! If you're not dressed properly you could be badly hurt, could be badly hurt."

"I don't care," said Roland. "Little Douglas can injure me all he likes."

Humphrey and Morris pushed and pummeled their roommate, dragging over his shoulders a mail shirt that hung down to his knees, pushing over his head a mail balaclava and covering his hands with steel gauntlets. They also found a basinet helmet that fitted perfectly, and slid a jouster's great helm over the top to cover Roland's whole face.

Roland looked at them through the eye slots. "I don't know why you're doing all this. I'm not even going to fight back."

His voice echoed in the helmet, but it lacked spark, and his knees were buckling under the weight of all the armor.

"Not going to fight back!" someone new

said deeply and loudly. "What's this non-sense?"

Roland couldn't see much through his great helm, but he knew straightaway that Sir Gallawood had arrived—even more so when a friendly punch on the shoulder almost sent him flying out the other side of the tent.

"Take off that lid, Roland. We must talk."

Roland uncovered his face with help from Humphrey and Morris, then slumped back to the ground. "I feel sadder than I've ever felt before, Sir Gallawood," he said in a tiny voice. "Maybe on another day I'd want to fight Little Douglas—if I could do it with a sword. Today I just want to go home."

"Roland, Roland, Roland," said Sir Gallawood. "The injury to Sir Lucas is sad. But we have to realize such things are the way of the world."

The constable's voice burst in from outside, hollering for "Master Wright."

Roland's face became very red. "Why do such things have to be the way of the world, Sir Gallawood? Why do good men have to be hurt?

"And you once said that if you are true to yourself, and fight nobly and justly, and as well as you possibly can, everything will work out for the best. I can't believe that Sir Lucas didn't do all that."

The constable roared again, "Master Wright, come out to fight."

Sir Gallawood stroked his pointy black beard and turned to Humphrey and Morris.

"Boys, go and tell the constable that Roland will be a few moments—and that he *will* take on Little Douglas."

Sir Gallawood turned back to Roland. "Sir Lucas was true to himself. I know it. He fought bravely, nobly and according to the code of chivalry. But we don't know what higher plans are made for us mere mortals. We have to believe in what we are doing, and we have to accept the risks that come with it.

"Being a knight, Roland, is a special gift. People like you and me are born with the fire within us. From the very first we feel the need to learn to fight, so we can protect our land, our loved ones and our King.

"And we need to compete in tournaments, even dangerous ones, to keep those important skills at their very utmost."

Roland wasn't entirely following Sir Gallawood's words, but something about his tone seemed to be making sense. And Roland realized that this smooth, deep voice reminded him of his own father. How he wished Oliver Wright could be here to tell him what to do.

Roland slowly pulled himself to his feet. "I don't think I could fight even a weakling right now, and Little Douglas is the most skillful boy I've ever seen."

Sir Gallawood looked down at Roland and put a huge hand on his shoulder, just as his father would have done. "It's at times like these, young man, that we learn who has what it takes to be a real knight. I believe you have what it takes, but do you?"

Roland didn't reply.

"Just before I came to this tent, Lady Mary said she wouldn't watch your fight with Little Douglas. I said she must. I said

that Roland Wright, her special page, was fighting for Sir Lucas, a fine knight, who sadly can't be here to finish his own jousting . . . a man who admires you, Roland, a man who told me he had never seen such speed, raw talent and determination in one of your age."

Humphrey and Morris arrived back, panting. "We told him, we told him. But when there are three short blasts of a trumpet, three short blasts of a trumpet, Roland must begin. He can't keep Their Majesties waiting, Their Majesties waiting."

Sir Gallawood turned back around. "The lances aren't sharp, Roland, so you can't be badly hurt. And it is not a question of whether you win or lose, it's about how you handle yourself in this difficult time. I know, Roland, that you can overcome your sadness. And I know you can be true to yourself.

"So will you fight, young man? Will you fight for Sir Lucas, for the King, for me, for your family? But most of all, will you fight to prove to yourself that you can do it—that you are Roland Wright, Future Knight?"

After a long silence, a tiny "Yes" stumbled from Roland's mouth. Immediately, three short blasts of a trumpet sounded outside.

The backs of Roland's legs were shaking. "Sir Gallawood, would you do one thing for me? Would you mind Nudge?"

Roland threw off one gauntlet, lifted Nudge and tried to put him into his cloth bag. But the nimble white mouse wriggled out of Roland's hand and ran up the inside of his sleeve of mail. He then jumped into the pocket behind Roland's breastplate.

Nudge was not going to leave Roland to face Little Douglas all on his own.

Nine

The Moment of Truth

Roland walked out into the sunshine to find that the pages of Twofold Castle had made a line of honor from the front of the tent all the way to the lists.

"Good luck," said the page with the helmet hair. "We don't think anyone can beat him, but we know you'll try hardest."

It was nice of the page to wish him luck, but Roland wasn't too sure about the rest of it. He was now very nervous. He didn't care about himself, but he didn't want Nudge to be hurt, or Sir Lucas to be let down.

Roland walked slowly along the line, hearing the phrase "Good luck" repeated by page after page. But at the end of the line

was Hector, still in his white shirt and smiling a nasty, toothy smile.

He too said "Good luck" but followed it

straightaway with "to Little Douglas, *s-s-s-s*." Hector laughed at Roland, then scoffed, "Not that he'll need any luck to flatten you, *peasant boy*."

The constable announced the rules— loudly. They were to joust on foot. The tilt-line had been lowered to waist height. There were to be three passes, the same as when jousting on horses.

Roland tried to listen to the rest of the rules, but there was so much else going through his mind. Each page had to present a fair target, the constable said.

"There is no ducking out of the way. You must give your best hit, and take their best hit. That is the chivalrous way to joust.

"The page who breaks the most lances shall win, unless one should knock the other to the ground. If that happens, the page still on his feet shall be the winner."

Back in his village, Roland had once run

at a spinning target, or quintain. But he had no other experience of jousting, and this lance was bigger, and heavier, too. Roland found it a struggle just to point it straight ahead with so much of the weight so far forward.

"What do you think you are doing, boy?" asked the constable impatiently.

"Holding the lance up?" Roland exhaled.

"Not with that hand, you're not, boy. The barrier is on your left, so you must hold the lance on your right. All lances have to be held in the right hand, otherwise it isn't fair and equal."

The constable

grabbed the lance and thrust the handle into Roland's other gauntlet. He pushed a small shield into Roland's left hand, saying, "You must carry that, too. Now hurry up!"

Using his right hand, Roland needed all his strength just to lift the tip of the lance off the ground. It was going to be hard enough to run with it, let alone aim it. Things didn't seem fair *or* equal.

While Roland stressed and strained, his opponent lifted his lance over his head and thrust it at imaginary targets. It looked as though jousting, for him, was the most normal thing in the world.

Roland hadn't seen Little Douglas's face, but before they were sent to opposite ends of the tiltline, he heard his voice.

"This is the moment of truth," the undefeated page said, with a surprisingly high-pitched tone for someone who moved so threateningly. "May the best page win!"

Roland tried to repeat "May the best page win," but his voice was so weak it couldn't make its way through the breathing holes on his great helm.

"Raise your lances to signal you are ready," rasped the constable. Roland was already sweating so much he could feel his armor sliding around. He heaved his lance up with his right hand, then began to run.

It was very hard to see Little Douglas through the bouncing eye slots. Roland couldn't hear the crowd, just the wind whistling through his helmet and the sound of his own breathing.

He decided that his only chance was to use his speed, and just before impact, he sped up even more. He dropped his lance tip at the last moment, but it missed completely.

Little Douglas's lance was spot on. Roland felt something like a hammer blow to his left shoulder. He only just managed to stay on his feet.

Roland could hear Nudge whimpering as the crowd cheered the breaking of Little Douglas's lance. "Jump out, Nudge," Roland growled through his pain, but his brave little mouse just pushed himself even more deeply into his pocket.

"One lance to Little Douglas," announced the constable, "and none to Roland Wright."

They lined up again and raised their lances. This time Roland was hit even harder and came closer to falling down. It felt as if he had run into a tree while sprinting as fast as he could.

"Two lances to Little Douglas," Sir Gallawood yelled to Roland. "The only way to win now is to knock him to the ground. I know you can do it."

"Yes, Roland, you can do it," blurted out

Sir Tobias, who was standing nearby. "I'd never be able to, but you can!"

Sir Geoffrey was watching too, and for a brief moment, it looked as though he might say something. But he didn't.

By the time Roland turned at the end of the tiltline, he was stumbling around dizzily. All the wind had been knocked out of him. Nudge, completely soaked in Roland's sweat, felt even worse. He'd twice been squashed between breastplate, mail shirt and chest.

"This is the last one, Nudge," Roland whispered. "Then we can both lie down."

Through his helmet Roland could hear a chant building up. He turned and saw Humphrey, Morris and almost all the other pages clapping their hands.

"COME ON, ROLAND! COME ON, ROLAND! COME ON . . ."

Even Nudge was bringing his front paws together in time with the pages. In the first two charges, Roland had been happy enough just to stay on his feet; he had never considered trying to do much more than that.

Now he could feel himself overcoming his sadness. He could sense that Sir Lucas was with him. In his mind he saw those green eyes and heard the words "There's no substitute for a huge heart."

The old fire was back. For the first time Roland wanted to win—and truly believed he could.

"I'm not even going to look at his lance this time, Nudge. I'm going to look only at where our lance has to go, because unless we knock him over, we won't win."

With that thought, Roland lifted his lance to signal he was ready for the last charge. He stuck out his bottom lip and started to run. As his feet moved under him, Roland suddenly remembered that, just before the collision each time, Little Douglas had lifted his head and looked at the sky. It was something many knights did to make sure no lance splinters poked through their eye slots.

Roland realized that, for a brief moment, his opponent couldn't see him. And this time, when Roland was just a few yards away from his opponent, he didn't speed up. Instead he slowed just a tiny bit.

Little Douglas's timing was thrown off by the change of pace, and his lance glanced harmlessly off the side of Roland's shield. While this happened, Roland watched the head go up, dropped his own lance and slid it right into Little Douglas's shoulder.

The impact was so great that Roland felt his lance shatter and his own arm jerk back so violently he feared he had broken it. Little Douglas disappeared from view, but Roland heard an enormous roar from the crowd.

He continued running along the tiltline, moving his right arm around to check it was still working. It seemed all right. He turned

to see Little Douglas lying flat on his back, with the broken end of Roland's lance sticking out of the shoulder joint in his armor.

"You did it!" yelled Sir Gallawood above the cheering of the pages, the clapping of the ladies and the roars of approval that were coming from the knights and even the King himself.

Nudge climbed out and jumped onto Roland's shoulder to soak up some of the applause.

The victor's thoughts, though, were not of triumph. He was worried he'd badly hurt Little Douglas, and he threw his shield and broken lance to the ground and ran as fast as he could.

The tip of the lance was wedged in the armor but hadn't pierced it. Roland was able to pull it out and open the front of the helmet. The opponent who had been so fearsome looked no older than Roland and had a small, freckly face so soft it could have been a girl's.

"Don't worry about me, I'll be all right," Little Douglas said, with a trickle of blood running from his nose. "It's only my pride that is really hurt. I didn't think any boy could beat me in any type of fighting, and certainly not one as young as you.

"I'll always remember your name, Roland Wright, and I'm sure we'll meet again."

At the end of the tourney, a long chain of people made their way back toward the castle.

As they walked in the line, Morris ran his hand slowly through his black hair and turned to Roland. "You did so well! I've heard they're going to make *you* the heir to the throne. Our next ruler: Mighty King Roland!"

There was no response. Roland cared only for finding out about Sir Lucas.

It was left to Humphrey to answer. "Don't be silly, Morris, don't be silly. That could never happen, never happen . . . could it?"

Ten

An Heir Is Announced

Jenny walked back with Lady Mary. As they crossed the fields near the castle, they caught up with Hector.

His head was cast down. He was kicking his feet forward slowly while moaning and hissing and grumbling to himself. "I wanted him hurt, s-s-s-s, really hurt. He wasn't meant to win!"

He didn't notice the woman and the young girl—until Jenny shouted at him.

"If you were chivalrous, Page Hector, you wouldn't let us walk through this muddy puddle ahead."

Hector looked up. He hissed and was ready to say something as rude as he possibly could to this friend of Roland. However, at the last moment he also saw Lady Mary and realized he had to be polite.

"I'm sorry, ladies, *s-s-s-s,* that I don't have a horse with which to carry you over the mud," said Hector, through gritted teeth.

"No matter," said Jenny. "A real knight

would simply take off his coat and use that to cover the puddle."

Lady Mary looked at Jenny with surprise, then slowly brought her handkerchief to her face to hide her growing smile.

"Unfortunately, *s-s-s-s*, I don't have a coat, either," said Hector, thinking himself very clever. "Otherwise I would be only too happy to cast my fine garment on the ground with no thought of anything but your well-being."

"Your shirt will do," Jenny snapped without out a moment's pause. "We ladies aren't proud."

Hector reddened and looked at Lady Mary, expecting her to tell Jenny to be quiet. Instead Lady Mary simply moved her hand-kerchief and echoed the words, "Yes, we ladies aren't proud."

Hector had no choice. With loud and unchivalrous groaning, grunting and hissing, he removed his new shirt—the whitest piece of clothing he had ever owned—and laid it across the filthy puddle.

Hector stood back and ungraciously held his hand out to usher the ladies forward. He waited for them to stamp his finest linen into the sludge.

"Look, Lady Mary!" Jenny suddenly cried out. "I've just seen a perfectly good path over there. Isn't that lucky—we can walk there instead."

With that, the two ladies strolled around the puddle—and Hector's shirt, which was

already turning brown as the mud seeped through it.

Hector was left shirtless and seething.

"S-s-s-s," he said. "S-s-s-s, s-s-s-s, s-s-s-s!"

Back at the castle, the bailey was cleared so that musicians, tumblers, jugglers and the jester could help welcome home the knights who had won their bouts.

Sir Tobias, his face a little bruised and bloody, had been unhorsed for the fourth time in his life, though he had broken his lance twice against one opponent. When he saw Roland step onto the drawbridge, he wiped his face clean and walked quickly toward him.

"I failed again, so no surprises there," said Sir Tobias, without leaving any spaces between the words. He grabbed Roland and pushed him into the queue of champions. "But you were victorious, young man, and should walk with the winners."

And so it was that Roland, with Nudge

on his shoulder, marched into the bailey between rows of colored banners and long lines of cheering spectators. The trumpets sounded, the people clapped and threw rose petals, the jugglers juggled and the tumblers tumbled. The Queen, her arm wrapped up in cloth after her collision with the tent, squinted when she saw Roland up close. She then screamed.

"John ... King John ... there's a mouse on that boy ... a mouse in the castle. Arrrrhh!"

Nudge responded by standing on his hind legs and waving his paws in her direction.

The crowd and music and jester's rhymes might have been exciting at some other time, but Roland was looking solely for somebody who could tell him what he most needed to hear. Lady Mary walked toward him with a silk handkerchief in her hand.

"How is Sir . . . ," Roland shouted above the crowd, but his voice trailed away. From the redness of Lady Mary's eyes, he knew things were bad.

"I'm so sorry, Roland," she said, but she was drowned out by a blaring of trumpets.

King John, wearing a long red and gold coat, walked onto a stage in the center of the bailey. He was followed closely by Lord Urbunkum, who was all the time coughing his little coughs.

"Congratulations to our brave knights

who fought so well," said the King, rubbing his beard and looking carefully at the lineup of champions. "Sadly, though, there were some serious injuries, and Sir Lucas, one of the finest knights any king has ever had by his side, is now fighting not for his team, the Tenans, but for his life."

The King took off his large jewel-studded crown and held it next to his chest. "My personal surgeon says that even if Sir Lucas doesn't succumb to his injuries, he may never walk again. For a knight, that's a fate worse than death. I've asked for a special Mass to pray for his recovery."

Roland felt tears on his cheeks as the King talked and Urbunkum coughed.

"This tournament, as you know, was special. My expert suggested it could be more than just training for war. It could be a way of selecting the noblest, bravest, strongest and most capable man to take over as King when I end my days. Such is my admiration for Lord Urbunkum, I agreed.

"I would now like him to explain more."

"Ahem," coughed Urbunkum as he puffed out his chest. "Yes, Your Majesties, knights, ladies and gentlemen of Twofold Castle, it was a terrific tournament. But, as the King said, there was tragedy as well as triumph. The tragedy was that Sir Lucas did not follow correctly the expert advice he was given. Fortunately, it could have been far worse."

Roland looked at Lord Urbunkum through his tears. He didn't know what to think, but an instant later someone nearby spoke up in a voice loud enough for everyone to hear.

"Far worse?"

blared Jenny. "What could be worse for a knight than to be almost killed and never able to walk again?"

The King scrunched up his eyes and looked ready to pounce down on Jenny. Urbunkum's eyes shrank and moved farther apart, while his whole head turned scarlet, as if about to explode.

Lady Mary quickly put an arm around Jenny and said loudly and clearly, "Your Majesty, she is newly orphaned and upset. She means no offense to you or your expert."

Urbunkum looked down as if Jenny were the most idiotic person imaginable. He placed his hands on his enormous stomach and sneered. "What could be worse? Not living . . . not living up to your potential, of course."

The King smiled at his expert's excellent answer. "I think that explains it clearly enough," he said. "On other matters, it will soon be time to announce the overall victor of our tournament and thereby pronounce the heir to the throne.

"As you all know, my firstborn son, Prince Daniel, was unable to compete, being only three years old. Fortunately, Urbunkum has been able to use his scientific methods to work out how Daniel would have fought if old enough, and to include him in the scoring system."

"Yes indeed, Your Majesty," said Urbunkum, who had calmed down as attention turned back to him. "I had to perform a difficult series of calculations, based not just on results, but on skills and style and, most importantly, on how well each competitor listened to the expert advice he was given.

"After all this complicated reckoning, the result was obvious. Prince Daniel was the clear winner, well ahead of Sir Geoffrey in second place."

Urbunkum coughed several more times, then announced, "And because of this tremendous result, Your Majesty, it's Prince Daniel who'll be appointed as your successor."

There was a huge cheer from all around the bailey, including from the knights—apart from Sir Geoffrey. He nodded a little bit and pulled on his nose but, as always, he said nothing.

The King congratulated Urbunkum on his fairness and expertise, then turned back to the crowd. "I wish to again mention the much-loved Sir Lucas. I command that we all now spend a moment in silence in his honor."

As the crowd responded, the only sounds to be heard were the wind whistling in the towers, the horses shuffling in the stables and the royal flag flapping above the gatehouse.

Roland looked at the drawbridge, which was still open. He felt sure Sir Lucas would walk through the arch at any moment, straightening a new silk scarf, twirling the end of his mustache between thumb and first finger and then lifting his hands to accept the cheers of the crowd and the admiration of the ladies.

But it didn't happen, and as the silence ended, people immediately started preparing for the banquet.

Roland was still looking around glumly when Sir Gallawood walked up and punched his right shoulder.

"I need to leave soon, young man," he said as Roland rubbed the top of his arm. "I wish Sir Lucas could have seen how well you fought. We all do.

"And we have to believe that Sir Lucas will recover, Roland, because there's no sense in thinking otherwise. Remember too that when something like this happens, we learn things that could be useful in real battles. So Sir Lucas wasn't injured for nothing."

Roland wasn't sure. Until now he'd always thought of fighting as something that was fun.

"There's another matter I want to discuss before I leave for my own castle," Sir Gallawood said while Roland moved a bit farther away, in case another friendly punch was in store. "I'm worried, Roland, about Jenny. She's here because I've personally asked the King, but she's very forthright. By that, I mean she says exactly what she thinks. That's a good thing—at times—but it can be dangerous in the King's castle. I need you to look out for her.

"And lastly, young Roland, remember that there'll be sad days ahead in your quest to be a knight. But there'll be happy and triumphant days too—and I know, in time, you'll join the very highest order of knights."

Sir Gallawood mounted his horse and rode toward the drawbridge. Roland loved

the idea of being in the very highest order of knights. But being badly hurt or watching your friends being badly hurt—or even killed—seemed a terrible price to pay.

As Sir Gallawood disappeared into the distance and the bailey slowly emptied, Roland sensed that everything was now just a little different. Humphrey, Morris and Jenny were coming over to take him to the banquet. He tried to walk away, but Morris and Jenny each put an arm around his shoulders, and

Humphrey lifted his finger and suggested a new couplet for their page's alphabet.

"S marks the sorrow we all feel this *day,* but T's for the true friends found on the *way.*"

Nudge looked at Humphrey, then turned to Roland.

"   ," Nudge added, in full agreement.

A Page's Alphabet

A is for armor, shiny and strong,

B is for battle, bloody and long,

C stands for castle, high on the hill,

D for the dragons we one day shall kill,

E is for effort, you must give your all,

and **F** is for fighting, in melee or brawl,

G stands for gauntlet, a steely great glove,

and **H** for the hunting that all good knights love,

I is for iron—to make a mail vest,

And J is for jousting, the ultimate test,

K is for king: a man strong, brave and wise,

L's for a longsword to cut you to size,

m is for mace, to be swung till they flee,

And n is for no one, 'cause that's who'll beat me,

O is for outlaws, to chase and to strike,

P's for a poleaxe, a page and a pike,

Q is for Queen, whom we greet on one knee,

R's for the robbers we smite when we see,

S stands for squire, for spurs
and for shield,

T's for a tourney where lesser
knights yield,

U is for unicorn, wondrous white steed,

V for the victory we one
day shall lead,

W's for warhorse, sturdy and fleet,

X marks the spot where the armies will meet,

Y's for the years that we count till we're knighted,

And **Z** means the end, and for that I'm delighted.

Acknowledgments

The author would like to dedicate this book to his wife, Carolyn Walsh, and his sons, William, James and Daniel. All read the manuscript and gave many excellent suggestions. (Okay, Daniel is three and prefers illustrations, but he did inspire a certain character in this story.)

Others read drafts and said things that made sense: Graham Harman, Glenn Morrison, Alison Peters, Matthew Hunyor, Tim Fitzpatrick, Ben Abberton, my brother Damian and my parents, Pedr and Dolores.

On the historical side, I've learned much from medieval reenactment groups, and am especially grateful to James Adams, Elden McDonald and other "Black Ravens" for sword-fighting lessons and more. Champion jouster Justin Holland gave me a wonderful grounding in the coolest extreme sport of 1409. But if there are historical anomalies in here, blame me and not them.

Lastly, my heartfelt appreciation to Gregory Rogers for rendering the characters, old and new, with such warmth, skill and dedication. It would be much less of a book without Gregory's contribution.

About the Author

Tony Davis has always worked with words. He has been a book publisher, magazine editor, and newspaper writer. In recent years he has been a full-time book author—his most difficult but most exciting job yet.

Tony has long been interested in knights and armor and the legends and stories of the Middle Ages. His enthusiasm for the period comes through clearly in the world of Roland Wright.

When he is not putting words on paper (or screens), Tony is playing football or cricket in the backyard with his sons, strumming a guitar, reading, hiking, or listening to music on his iPod, stereo, or hand-cranked 78-rpm record player.

About the Illustrator

Gregory Rogers studied fine art at the Queensland College of Art and has illustrated a large number of educational and trade children's picture books. He won the Kate Greenaway Medal for his illustrations in *Way Home*.

His first wordless picture book, *The Boy, The Bear, The Baron, The Bard,* was selected as one of the *New York Times* Ten Best Illustrated Children's Books of the Year and received numerous other awards and nominations. He also illustrated *Midsummer Knight,* the companion to *The Boy, The Bear, The Baron, The Bard.*